To Kristen with love on
2nd birthday, from Aunt Eileen, Uncle
Mike, Stacey & Camille.

LITTLE PEOPLE'S MOTHER GOOSE

LITTLE PEOPLE'S

Pictures by JENI BASSETT

MOTHER GOOSE

Compiled by BARBARA LUCAS

DERRYDALE BOOKS
New York

Copyright © 1988 by Lucas/Evans Books
Illustrations © 1988 by Jeni Bassett
All rights reserved.

This 1988 edition is published by Derrydale Books, distributed by
Crown Publishers, Inc., 225 Park Avenue South, New York, New York 10003

Printed and bound in Italy

Library of Congress Cataloging-in-Publication Data

Little people's Mother Goose.
    Summary: An illustrated collection of traditional rhymes.
    1. Nursery rhymes. 2. Children's poetry. [1. Nursery
rhymes] I. Bassett, Jeni, ill. II. Title.
PZ8.3.L7333 1988   398'.8   87-27261
ISBN 0-517-65860-7

h g f e d c b a

For the Appletons
—B.L.

For Jennifer and Rachel
—J.B.

CONTENTS

LEARNING RHYMES AND RIDDLES 33

OLD FRIENDS AND FAVORITES 47

LITTLE
RHYMES
ABOUT
LITTLE
PEOPLE

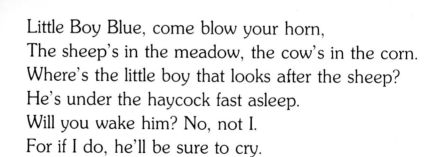

Little Boy Blue, come blow your horn,
The sheep's in the meadow, the cow's in the corn.
Where's the little boy that looks after the sheep?
He's under the haycock fast asleep.
Will you wake him? No, not I.
For if I do, he'll be sure to cry.

Little Betty Blue
Lost her holiday shoe.
What shall little Betty do?
Buy her another
To match the other,
And then she'll walk in two.

15

Little Jack Horner
Sat in a corner,
Eating a Christmas pie.
He put in his thumb
And pulled out a plum,
And said, "What a good boy am I!"

Little Miss Muffett
Sat on a tuffet,
Eating her curds and whey.
There came a great spider
And sat down beside her,
And frightened Miss Muffett away.

Little Bo-peep has lost her sheep,
And can't tell where to find them.
Leave them alone, and they'll come home,
And bring their tails behind them.

SONGS
AND
GAMES

Three blind mice! Three blind mice!
See how they run! See how they run!
They all ran after the farmer's wife,
Who cut off their tails with the carving knife,
Did you ever see such fun in your life?
As three blind mice.

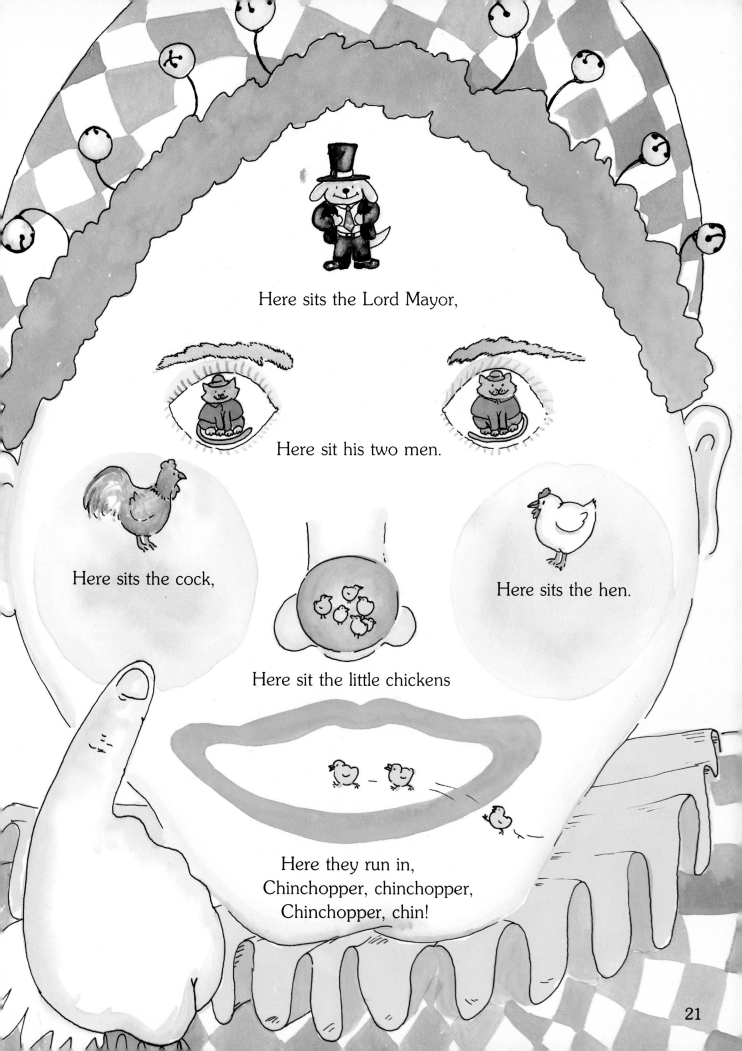

Here sits the Lord Mayor,

Here sit his two men.

Here sits the cock,

Here sits the hen.

Here sit the little chickens

Here they run in,
Chinchopper, chinchopper,
Chinchopper, chin!

Pat-a-cake, pat-a-cake, baker's man!
Make me a cake as fast as you can.
Prick it, and stick it, and mark it with a B,
And put it in the oven for Baby and me.

Hush-a-bye, baby, on the tree top,
When the wind blows, the cradle will rock.
When the bough breaks, the cradle will fall,
Down will come baby, and cradle, and all.

Here we go round the mulberry bush,
The mulberry bush, the mulberry bush,
Here we go round the mulberry bush,
On a cold and frosty morning.

This little pig went to market,

This little pig stayed home,

This little pig had roast beef,

This little pig had none.

This little pig said, "Wee, wee, wee!"
All the way home.

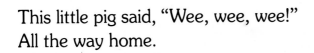

1 This pig went to the barn,
2 This ate all the corn.
3 This said he would tell,
4 This said he wasn't well.
5 This went week, week, week, over the door sill.

I am a gold lock.
I am a gold key.

I am a silver lock.
I am a silver key.

I am a brass lock.
I am a brass key.

I am a lead lock.
I am a lead key.

I am a monk lock.
I am a monk key!

1 I went up one pair of stairs.
2 Just like me.

1 I went up two pair of stairs.
2 Just like me.

1 I went into a room.
2 Just like me.

1 I looked out of the window.
2 Just like me.
1 And there I saw a monkey.
2 Just like me.

One for the money,
Two for the show,
Three to make ready,
And four to go!

London Bridge is falling down,
Falling down, falling down.
London Bridge is falling down,
My fair lady.

Ring a ring o' roses,
A pocketful of posies,
Tisha! Tisha!
We all fall down.

Peter, Peter, pumpkin eater,
Had a wife and couldn't keep her.
He put her in a pumpkin shell,
And there he kept her very well.

Peter, Peter, pumpkin eater,
Had another and didn't love her.
Peter learned to read and spell,
And then he loved her very well.

LEARNING
RHYMES
AND
RIDDLES

January brings the snow,
Makes our feet and fingers glow.

February brings the rain,
Thaws the frozen lake again.

March brings breezes loud and shrill,
Stirs the dancing daffodil.

April brings the primrose sweet,
Scatters daisies at our feet.

May brings flocks of pretty lambs,
Skipping by their fleecy dams.

June brings tulips, lilies, roses,
Fills the children's hands with posies.

Hot July brings cooling showers,
Apricots and gillyflowers.

August brings the sheaves of corn.
Then the harvest home is borne.

Warm September brings the fruit.
Sportsmen then begin to shoot.

Fresh October brings the pheasant.
Then to gather nuts is pleasant.

Dull November brings the blast.
Then the leaves are whirling fast.

Chill December brings the sleet,
Blazing fire and Christmas treat.

Two legs sat upon three legs,
With one leg in his lap.
In comes four legs,
Runs away with one leg.
Up jumps two legs,
Catches up three legs,
Throws it after four legs,
And makes him bring back one leg.

Thirty days hath September,
April, June, and November.
February has twenty-eight alone,
All the rest have thirty-one,
Excepting leap year—that's the time
When February's days are twenty-nine.

One, two, three, four,
Mary at the cottage door.
Five, six, seven, eight,
Eating cherries off a plate.
O–U–T spells out!

Apple pie, pudding, and pancake,
All begins with A.

A, apple pie.
B bit it,

C cut it,
D dealt it

E ate it,
F fought for it,

G got it,
H had it,

I inspected it,
J joined it,
K kept it,

L longed for it,
M mourned for it,

N nodded at it,
O opened it,

P peeped in it,
Q quartered it,

R ran for it,
S stole it,

T took it,
V viewed it,

W wanted it,
X, Y, Z, and &
All wished for a piece in hand.

A, B, C, tumble down D.
The cat's in the cupboard and can't see me.

Long legs, crooked thighs,
Little head and no eyes.

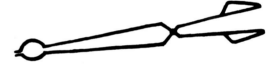

Old mother Twitchett had but one eye,
And a long tail which she let fly.
And every time she went over a gap,
She left a bit of her tail in a trap.

Little Nancy Etticoat,
In a white petticoat
And a red nose.
The longer she stands,
The shorter she grows.

A house full, a hole full,
And you cannot gather a bowl full.

Higher than a house,
Higher than a tree,
Oh, whatever can that be?

43

How many days has my baby to play?
Saturday, Sunday, Monday.
Tuesday, Wednesday, Thursday, Friday,
Saturday, Sunday, Monday.

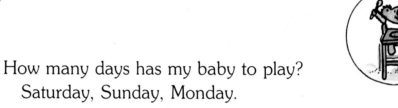

March winds and April showers
Bring forth May flowers.

Elizabeth, Elspeth, Betsy, and Bess,
They all went together to seek a bird's nest.
They found a bird's nest with five eggs in.
They all took one, and left four in.

OLD
FRIENDS
AND
FAVORITES

Georgie Porgie, pudding and pie,
Kissed the girls and made them cry.
When the girls come out to play,
Georgie Porgie runs away.

There was an old woman who lived in a shoe.
She had so many children she didn't know what to do.
She gave them some broth without any bread,
She whipped them all round, and sent them to bed.

49

Humpty Dumpty sat on a wall,
Humpty Dumpty had a great fall.
All the king's horses and all the king's men
Could not put Humpty Dumpty together again.

50

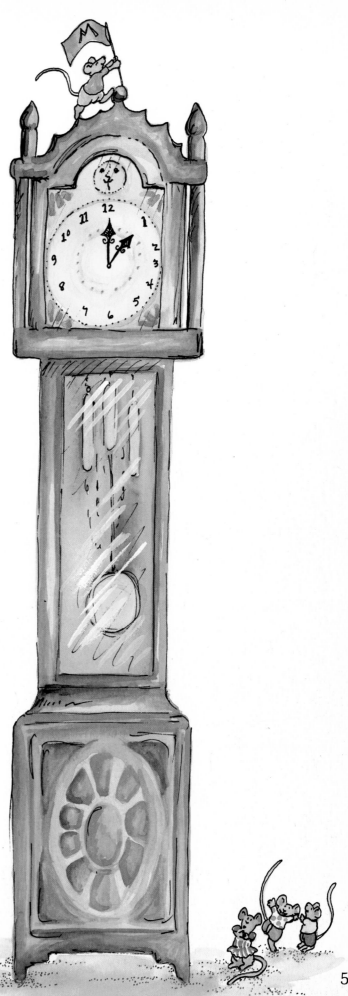

Hickory, dickory, dock,
The mouse ran up the clock.
The clock struck one,
The mouse ran down,
Hickory, dickory, dock.

Hey! diddle, diddle,
The cat and the fiddle,
The cow jumped over the moon.
The little dog laughed
To see such craft,
And the dish ran away with the spoon.

Baa, baa, black sheep,
Have you any wool?
Yes, sir, yes, sir,
Three bags full.

One for my master,
And one for my dame,
And one for the little boy
Who lives in our lane.

Jack Sprat could eat no fat,
His wife could eat no lean.
And so betwixt them both,
They licked the platter clean.

There was an old woman tossed up in a basket,
Nineteen times as high as the moon.
Where she was going I couldn't but ask it,
For in her hand she carried a broom.

"Old woman, old woman, old woman," quoth I,
"Oh whither, oh whither, oh whither so high?"
"To brush the cobwebs off the sky!"
"Shall I go with thee?" "Aye, by and by."

Old Mother Hubbard,
She went to the cupboard,
To get her poor dog a bone,
But when she came there,
The cupboard was bare,
And so the poor dog had none.

Yankee Doodle went to town
Upon a little pony.
He stuck a feather in his hat,
And called it Macaroni.

Mary, Mary,
Quite contrary,
How does your garden grow?
With silver bells,
And cockleshells,
And pretty maids all in a row.

To market, to market,
To buy a plum bun,
Home again, home again,
Market is done.

Jack be nimble,
Jack be quick,
Jack jump over the candlestick.

Wee Willie Winkie runs through the town,
Upstairs and downstairs in his nightgown.
Rapping at the window, crying through the lock,
"Are the children in their beds? For now it's eight o'clock."